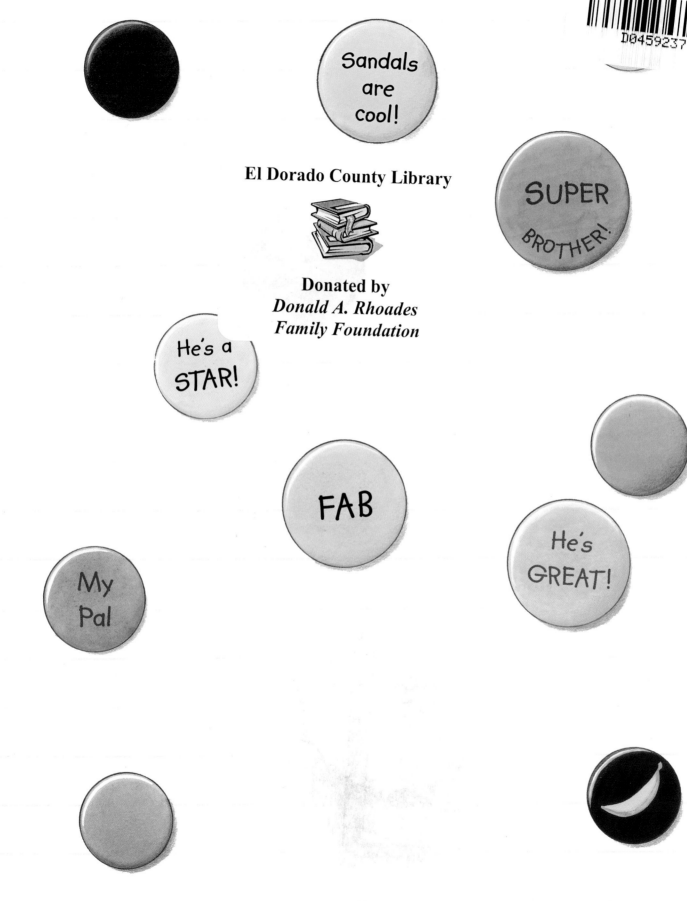

Sandals are cool!

SUPER BROTHER!

He's a STAR!

FAB

My Pal

He's GREAT!

To my brother, Michael, who isn't cool! (He's warm!)

Library of Congress Cataloging-in-Publication Data
Browne, Anthony, date.
My brother / Anthony Browne.— 1st American ed.
p.   cm.
Summary: A child describes the many wonderful things
about "my brother," who can fly, write amazing stories, and
stand up to bullies.
ISBN-13: 978-0-374-35120-5
ISBN-10: 0-374-35120-1
[1. Brothers—Fiction.]   I. Title.

PZ7.B81984 Mxt 2007
[E]—dc22   2006050262

With thanks to
Iona Scott's class at
the British School
in the Netherlands
for inspiring this book

Anthony Browne
MY BROTHER

Farrar Straus Giroux • New York

My brother
is really COOL.

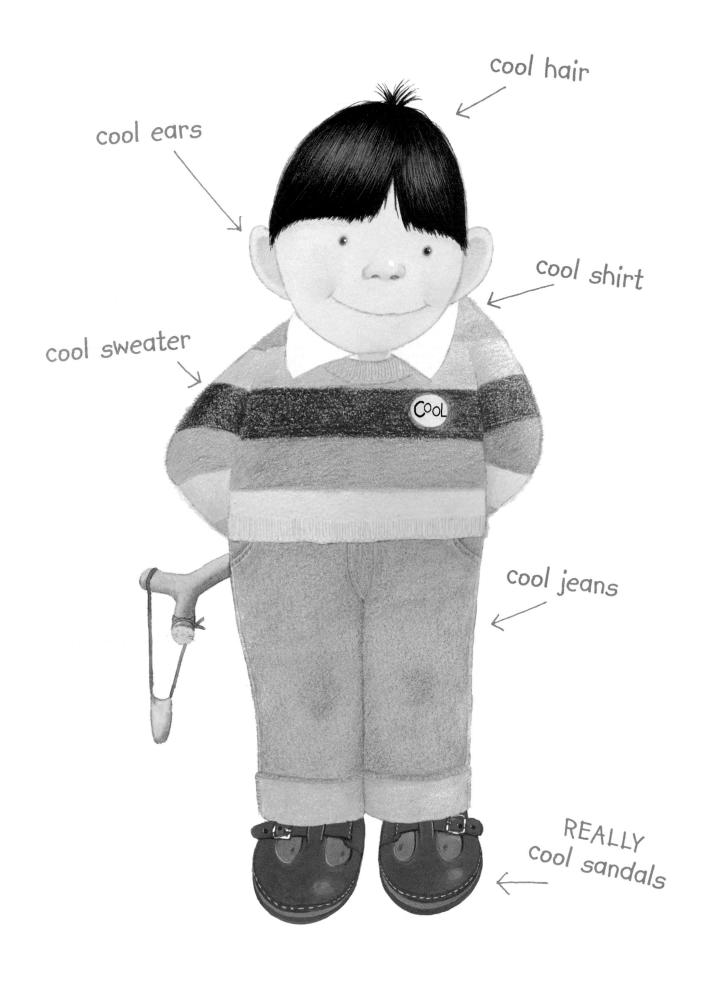

He's a GREAT jumper,

cool jump

cool climbing

cool Kong

a
TERRIFIC
climber,

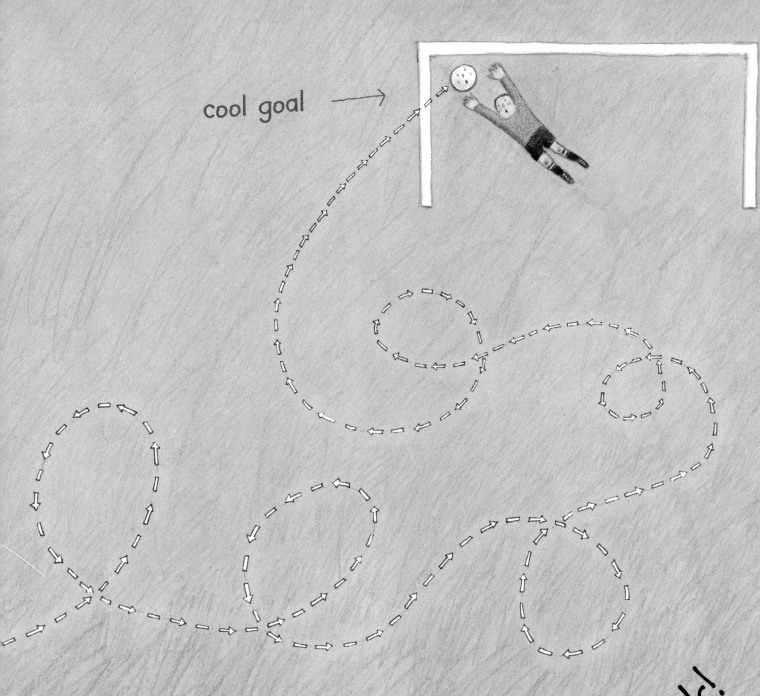

cool goal →

and he scores FANTASTIC goals!

He's REALLY cool, my brother.

My brother's a SUPER skateboarder,

cool boxers →

and he's got
MASSIVE
muscles.

He can run so FAST that...

...he can FLY!

Yes, my brother
is really COOL.

cool
chair →

My brother's read
HUNDREDS of books,

cool
Knight

cool giant

cool soldier

and he writes
BRILLIANT stories.

He can draw
ANYTHING,

cool wolf
←

and he can blow AMAZING bubbles.
He's REALLY COOL, my brother.

very cool mike

cool haircut

My brother is a WILD rock singer,

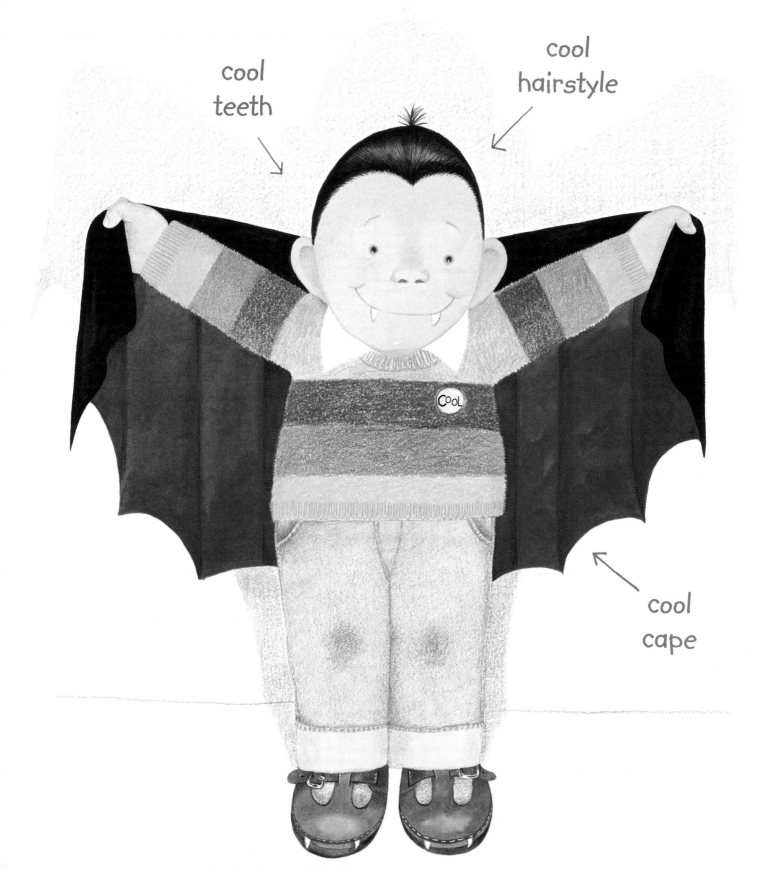

Sometimes he can be VERY SCARY,

and he can even WHISTLE!
My brother is SO cool.

My brother STANDS UP to bullies,

and SITS DOWN
on monsters.

As a matter of fact, my brother
is a REAL COOL CAT.

And guess what . . .

I'M COOL, TOO!

cool
ears

cool hair

cool
sweater

cool shirt

COOL

cool
jeans

cool sandals

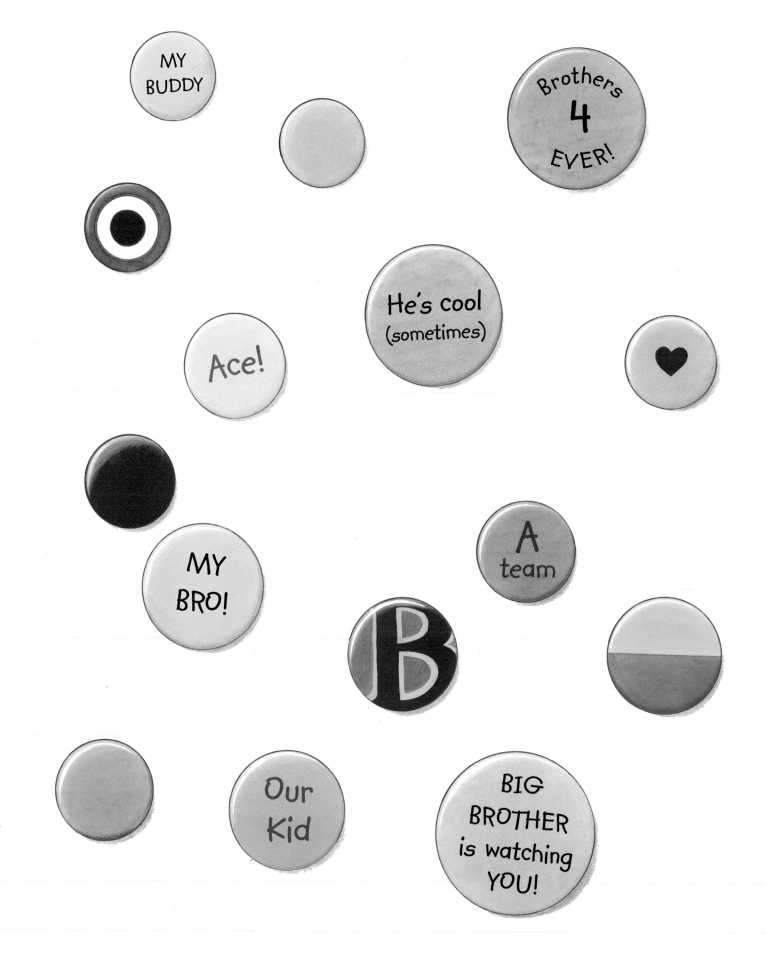